Kilmer's Pet Monster

There are more books about the Bailey City Monsters!

Kilmer's Pet Monster

by **Marcia Thornton Jones**
and
Debbie Dadey

illustrated by **John Steven Gurney**

A
LITTLE APPLE
PAPERBACK

SCHOLASTIC INC.
New York   Toronto   London   Auckland   Sydney

*To Barbara and Lee Beckham and their
pet monster, Pistol Pete.—MTJ*

For Kevin Gibson, a great nephew—DD

ISBN 0-590-10847-6

Text copyright © 1998 by Marcia Thornton Jones and Debra S. Dadey.
Illustrations copyright © 1998 by Scholastic Inc.
All rights reserved. Published by Scholastic Inc.
LITTLE APPLE PAPERBACKS is a trademark of Scholastic Inc.
THE ADVENTURES OF THE BAILEY SCHOOLS KIDS in design is
a registered trademark of Scholastic Inc.

12 11 10 9 8 7   4 5 6 / 8 9/0

Printed in the U.S.A.   40

First Scholastic printing, June 1998

Contents

1

Hocus Pocus Visitor

"What took you so long?" Jane asked Ben and Annie. "We're going to be late for school." Jane had been waiting for Annie and her older brother, Ben, in front of their house for at least ten minutes. They always walked to school together.

Annie pointed to Ben. "Ben couldn't find his math book."

Ben started to argue but Jane stepped between them. "We don't have time for a fight," she said as she led them to the house next door. "Let's get Kilmer."

It wasn't too long ago that the house at 13 Dedman Street was brand-new. Then the Hauntlys moved in. Now the paint was cracked and the lawn was crispy brown. All the trees in the yard were dead sticks, and the inn's shutters hung at crazy angles. A

1

lopsided sign that said HAUNTLY MANOR INN creaked in the morning breeze.

"This place looks worse every day," Annie said.

Ben shrugged. "I think it's cool."

"It doesn't matter how it looks," Jane reminded them. "But it does matter if we're late for school."

The three friends made their way up the cracked sidewalk. Just as they started climbing the steps, a stranger stepped out from the shadows of the porch. The three kids took a giant step back and looked up into the wrinkled face of the strange lady.

She wore a long black robe and pointy black shoes. Except for silver streaks, even her long frizzy hair was black. She held a broom, but she didn't look as if she planned to sweep any of the cobwebs hanging from the railing. Instead, she propped the broom against the house and smiled, showing crooked yellow teeth.

"Good morning, my little ones," the stranger said.

Ben stared and Annie gulped, but Jane held out her hand. "You must be the Hauntlys' newest guest," she said. "My name is Jane. Did you just get here?"

When the old woman shook Jane's hand, Annie noticed the old woman's nails were painted a sickly shade of green. "I flew in last night," the stranger said, "by the light of the moon. I am Priscilla Pocus."

"My name is Annie and this is my brother, Ben," Annie said politely. "We live next door. Welcome to Bailey City."

Just then Sparky leaped onto the porch railing. Sparky was Kilmer's pet cat, but she was anything but tame. The kids were used to the way Sparky hissed and darted around Hauntly Manor as if ghosts had her by the tail.

"The first thing you should know," Ben warned Priscilla, "is not to pet that cat. She has long claws and she's not afraid to use them."

Priscilla's laugh gave Annie a serious case of goose bumps. "Sparky doesn't scare me," Priscilla said. *"Feline claws, whiskers, and fur. I'll scratch your chin and hear you purr."*

The old lady finished her rhyme then reached out a single green fingernail to scratch Sparky's chin. The kids could hear Sparky's rumbling purr all the way across the porch.

"Wow," Ben said. "I've never seen Sparky let anyone except Kilmer get close to her."

"I didn't think Sparky knew how to purr," Jane added.

Priscilla laughed again. Annie noticed that the old lady's laugh sounded like paper being crumpled. "I have a way with cats," Priscilla said.

"I wish we could stay to talk more," Jane said. "But we're late for school. We came to get Kilmer."

"I will get him for you," Priscilla said. Sparky hopped off the railing and rubbed against the stranger's leg. Priscilla pointed to an old rocking chair and looked at Sparky. *Hop in that chair. I won't be long, wait for me there.* The words were barely out of her mouth when Sparky jumped in the chair and curled into a little ball. Then Priscilla Pocus disappeared inside Hauntly Manor Inn.

"I can't believe it," Ben said. "That cat is acting so friendly."

"I wouldn't get too close to Sparky," Jane warned. "She may like Priscilla, but she still thinks we're walking, talking scratching posts."

"It's strange seeing Sparky act calm," Ben said.

"Sparky's not the strangest thing we've seen this morning," Annie said.

"Everything is strange about Hauntly Manor Inn," Jane said with a laugh.

Annie nodded. "But I think things just got a little stranger," she said, "when Priscilla Pocus flew into town."

Annie couldn't say any more because just then the door to Hauntly Manor Inn slowly creaked open.

2

Pet Show

Kilmer stepped onto the porch. Kilmer was in the fourth grade with Jane and Ben, but he was at least a foot taller. With his heavy brown shoes and flattop haircut, Annie thought their friend looked just like Frankenstein's monster, especially today because his shirt was torn in three places.

"What happened to you?" Ben asked. "It looks like a tiger played tug-of-war with your shirt."

Kilmer glanced down at his shirt. "I was playing with Bruno," he said. "It was so much fun, I forgot about the time."

"Who is Bruno?" Annie asked.

"Priscilla's pet," Kilmer told her. "He likes it in our basement because it reminds him of the cave where he usually lives."

"What kind of pet lives in a cave?" Ben asked.

"You can tell us about Bruno later," Jane interrupted. "We have to hurry or we'll be late for school."

The four kids raced down Dedman Street toward Bailey Elementary School. "I think we made it on time," Annie said. "There's still a bunch of kids on the playground." She pointed to a crowd of third-graders gathered under a giant oak tree.

"I wonder what they're doing," Jane said.

"There's only one way to find out," Ben told them. He raced toward the oak tree. Annie, Jane, and Kilmer ran after him.

A boy named Howie stood in the middle of the crowd of kids. He held a purple piece of paper. "When is it?" a girl named Liza asked him.

Howie looked at the paper and read, "The Bailey City Pet Contest will be held this Saturday in Bailey City Park. A brand-new bicycle will be awarded to the owners of the most unusual and talented pet."

"All right!" a boy named Eddie yelled. "I'm entering my aunt's dog. Diamond is sure to win a pet contest."

Carey lived near Ben, Annie, Jane, and Kilmer. She stepped in front of Eddie and shook her head so hard her blond curls bounced. "My poodle is better than your aunt's Dalmatian," she said.

"My parrot is more talented than both of your stupid dogs," a girl named Issy bragged. "I'll win that bicycle."

"Are there any rules?" a third-grader named Melody asked before a fight broke out.

Howie nodded. "All pets must be well-trained and able to get along with other pets. They must be on a leash or in a cage."

The kids all started talking at once. Everyone was planning on entering their pets.

Ben, Annie, Kilmer, and Jane walked toward the school door. "I sure would like to have a new bicycle," Ben said. "Mine is all banged up."

"At least you have one," Annie pointed out. "Kilmer doesn't have a bike."

"He could enter his cat," Jane said with a giggle. "Maybe Sparky wouldn't bite off the judge's hand."

Ben shook his head. "Howie's paper said the prize would be given to an unusual pet. I think Kilmer should enter Minerva, Winifred, and Elvira." The kids knew all about Kilmer's three pet spiders. Kilmer had studied the patterns of their webs for the fourth-grade science fair. "I'm going to

talk Mom into letting me get a big iguana so I can enter the contest, too," Ben added.

"Don't bother," Jane said with a laugh. "I plan on winning that contest."

"How?" Annie said. "You don't have a pet."

"Easy," Jane told them. "I'll put a leash around Ben's neck and tell everyone he's my pet ape."

"That won't work," Annie said. "He isn't smart enough to learn any tricks."

"Very funny, monkey breath," Ben said.

"Wait!" Kilmer yelled, interrupting his friends. "I have a better idea."

"What could be better than creepy-crawly spiders?" Ben asked.

Kilmer smiled. "Priscilla's pet," he told them. "Bruno is most unusual. Bailey City has never seen anything like him."

Annie pulled on Jane's sleeve. "What kind of pet would Priscilla have?" Annie whispered.

"If Kilmer thinks it's unusual, then it can only be one thing," Jane said slowly. "A pet monster."

3
Pet Spies

By Friday afternoon, every kid at Bailey Elementary was busy getting ready for the pet show. Ben, Annie, Jane, and Kilmer stood on the playground and watched Eddie with his aunt's dog. He was trying to get the Dalmatian to walk, sit, and heel, but Prince Diamond was too busy chasing squirrels and dragging Eddie along behind him.

Carey laughed and reached down to straighten the bow on her poodle's head. Then Carey and her poodle pranced by Ben, Annie, Jane, and Kilmer.

"It's no fair," Ben complained. "Mom won't let me get an iguana. Everybody else has a cool pet except me."

Annie tapped her brother on the shoulder. "I don't have a pet."

"Me, neither," Jane added.

"You two don't count," Ben grumbled.

"Why can't you get a lizard?" Kilmer asked.

"Mom said they're too creepy," Ben said.

Kilmer looked confused. "But lizards are cuddly," he argued.

"Not according to my mom," Annie said.

"I'll be the only kid that doesn't have a chance to win that new bike," Ben grumbled.

"You could borrow Minerva, Winifred, and Elvira," Kilmer said.

Ben slapped Kilmer on the back. "Do you mean it?" Ben asked. "You'd really let me borrow your spiders?"

"Of course," Kilmer said. "They like you. I'm sure they wouldn't mind."

"Then we have to hurry home," Ben said. "I have lots of work to do."

The four kids ran toward Dedman Street. On the way, they passed Issy's house. Issy sat on her porch, a parrot perched on her shoulder.

"Hey!" Issy called. "Don't you want to stop and see what my parrot can do? I've been training Filbert for the pet show."

Ben would have kept running except Annie reached out and grabbed his elbow. "Be nice," she whispered. "Issy doesn't have many friends."

Ben shrugged. "That's because nobody likes her," he said matter-of-factly.

"We should see what she's training her pet to do," Jane pointed out.

"Are you talking about spying?" Ben asked.

Jane nodded. "It might help you win the contest."

Ben grinned. "Why didn't you say so in the first place? Let's go do some pet spying."

The four friends walked up the sidewalk and stopped in front of Issy. Isabel Hart was in the fourth grade with Ben, Kilmer, and Jane, but she thought she was the prettiest girl in all of Bailey City. Ben tried to stay as far away from her as possible.

"We'd love to see what your bird can do," Jane said.

The parrot's bright green wings fluttered. "Filbert want a cracker?" Issy asked the bird.

Filbert looked at Issy. He cocked his head to one side and said, "Awk!"

"Is that it?" Ben blurted. "You trained your bird to say awk?"

Issy huffed. "I just started. By tomorrow he'll be talking up a storm," she told them. "I'll win that bicycle and you won't win a thing."

"And the sky will turn purple," Ben said with a laugh.

"You're just jealous," Issy told Ben, "because you don't have a pet to enter in the contest."

Ben stood up tall. "I do too. And so does Kilmer. Our pets are much better than yours."

"What are they?" Issy asked, a worried look on her face.

Kilmer spoke before Ben had a chance. "It's a surprise," he said.

Ben nodded. "You won't find out until tomorrow," he told her.

But as the four friends walked away from Issy's house, Ben grabbed Kilmer's arm. "If Issy really gets her featherbrained bird to talk, we'll be in trouble," he said. "We have to train our pets to do something special, just in case."

Kilmer nodded. "That won't be a problem. Bruno is very talented. He can do things no other pet can do."

"Are you sure?" Jane asked. "After all, we haven't even seen him."

Kilmer scratched his head and sighed. "Bruno is a bit shy," Kilmer said. "He's not used to being around people."

"Are you sure he's safe?" Annie asked.

Kilmer thought for a moment. "It will be safe," he finally said.

"I hope you're right," Jane said, "or the people of Bailey City may be in for the surprise of their lives!"

4
Hauntly Pet Tricks

Kilmer's parents sat on the porch when the kids reached Hauntly Manor Inn. Kilmer's father, Boris Hauntly, smiled, showing his pointy eyeteeth. Boris was very tall and always wore a black cape. If it wasn't for his red hair, Boris would be a dead ringer for Dracula. "Would you like to come in for an after-school treat?" Boris asked.

Kilmer's mother, Hilda Hauntly, smiled. "We just finished baking some delicious peanut butter and worm cookies." Hilda was a scientist and stirred up unusual inventions, but her cooking inventions were the strangest of all. Jane, Ben, and Annie were never brave enough to try any of the Hauntlys' recipes.

"No thank you," Ben said. "I have to get

ready for the pet show. Kilmer is letting me borrow his spiders."

"And we're going to help him," Jane said quickly.

Kilmer nodded. "Bruno must know how to do tricks if I am to win."

Boris smiled. "Teaching Bruno tricks sounds like fun. Perhaps you can teach him to swoop down and grab furry creatures in his claws."

Hilda nodded. "Or Bruno could learn how to open his jaws wide so the judge can stick his head inside."

"But what if he makes a mistake and closes his mouth?" Annie asked.

"Hmmm, that could be a little messy," Hilda agreed. "Will there be any spare judges on hand?"

"I'm not sure," Annie said. "Maybe Kilmer should try teaching Bruno something else."

"Before I do anything," Kilmer interrupted, "I have to get Bruno to stay on a leash."

Boris' eyes opened wide. "I don't think Bruno has ever been on a leash before," he said. "Are you sure it can be done?"

"He has to be on a leash," Ben told Boris. "It's one of the rules."

Hilda stood up. "Perhaps we should help," she said. "After all, Bruno isn't used to cooperating."

Boris nodded. "We will meet you in the basement," he told Kilmer. "Perhaps the three of us can tame Bruno." Hilda and Boris opened the door and entered the darkness of Hauntly Manor Inn.

"Bruno sounds big," Annie said.

"And mean," Jane added.

Kilmer shrugged. "He's not so bad once he gets to know you."

"I think I'll stick to spiders," Ben said. "I'll try training them while you work with Bruno."

Kilmer nodded. "I'll get them for you." Kilmer left Ben, Annie, and Jane alone on the porch.

"I hope Kilmer knows what he's doing," Annie said.

Jane nodded. "If Bruno is half the monster I think he is," she said slowly, "we may be in big trouble!"

5

Spider Tricks

"What are you doing?" Jane asked Ben. Jane and Annie were sitting on the Hauntlys' porch steps, waiting for Kilmer, while Ben was doing a headstand on the grass.

"I'm trying to teach these spiders some tricks," Ben explained.

Annie giggled. "I don't think spiders can learn to stand on their heads," she said.

"Sure they can," Ben told her. "You two stand on your heads and help me."

"Not in your lifetime," Jane said and scooted farther away from the three glass spider cases. She moved back toward the window and startled Sparky. Sparky was stretched out on the windowsill and did not look pleased at being disturbed.

"Maybe you could teach them another

trick," Annie suggested. "Like diving into a glass of water."

"Do spiders like water?" Jane asked.

"Who cares?" Ben asked, grabbing Sparky's water dish and sliding it into Minerva's case. "It would be a neat trick."

Jane watched Minerva scamper away from the black bowl. "Minerva doesn't seem too interested," Jane said.

"It's not fair," Ben complained. "If Mom had let me get an iguana I wouldn't have this problem."

"I know," Jane said, giggling. "Why don't you climb to the top of the roof and jump headfirst into the little water bowl yourself? Maybe Minerva just needs to see you do it."

"Very funny," Ben said with a sneer. "I hope Minerva has babies and they all come to live in your underwear."

"Don't get mad," Annie told her brother. "Maybe you just need to keep trying."

"I could try until my teeth rot," Ben

grumbled. "These spiders don't want to do anything exciting."

HISSSSSS! GRRRRRR! RRROAAARRR!

"I don't think Minerva made that noise," Annie said with a gulp.

"It wasn't me," Ben said.

Jane looked toward the Hauntlys' basement window. "It sounded to me like it came from the basement."

HISSSSSS! GRRRRRRR!

"Maybe we should go home," Annie said, quickly jumping up from the porch.

"I think we should check it out," Ben said.

"Didn't Kilmer say that Bruno was in the basement?" Jane asked.

Annie nodded and her eyes got really wide. "What if Bruno ate Hilda, Boris, and Kilmer?"

"Don't be silly," Jane said. "I'm sure that could never happen. At least, I don't think so."

"What if they need help?" Annie asked.

"I know how to find out," Ben said, running over to the basement window.

"You shouldn't spy on our neighbors," Annie scolded.

Ben ignored Annie, stooped down by the basement window, and peered in.

"Maybe Ben is right. We should check on the Hauntlys," Jane said. "Just to make sure they're okay."

Annie nodded and the two girls joined Ben at the basement window. "I can't see anything," Annie complained. "The window is too grimy."

"Shhh," Jane said. "I hear something."

GRRRRRR! HISSSSSS! RROOAARR!

"I don't like the sound of this," Annie whispered. "We should get out of here before it's too late."

"It is already too late," said a voice from behind them. All three kids turned to stare into the crooked yellow teeth of Priscilla Pocus.

6
What a Trick!

"What are my pretty little ones doing?" Priscilla Pocus asked.

Annie gulped, but Jane didn't hesitate. "We were trying to teach Kilmer's spiders to do tricks when we heard horrible noises coming from the basement."

"We thought Kilmer might be in danger from Bruno," Ben told Priscilla.

Priscilla laughed a funny cackling laugh. "Bruno would not hurt my little Kilmer. What is this about teaching spiders tricks?"

"Ben tried to teach them to stand on their heads," Annie explained. "He didn't have any luck."

"Let's take a look at these stubborn spiders," Priscilla suggested. Priscilla glided over to the porch and stared at the glass

cases. She clapped her hands and said a little rhyme:

"Spinning webs and flies don't dread. Now, my sweeties, stand on your head."

"Oh, my gosh," Annie squealed. "It worked! The spiders are actually flipping over."

"That's not all," Jane said to Annie. "Look at Sparky." Sparky came running around the corner of the house and landed on her head. Then she stood up and rubbed Priscilla's leg.

Ben cheered, still watching the spiders. "All right! Just wait until Prissy Issy sees this!"

Annie crossed her arms and looked at Priscilla Pocus. "How did you do that?" Annie asked.

Priscilla smiled, showing her yellow teeth. "It's nothing really," she said. "I just have a way with creatures."

"You sure do," Ben said. "Do you think you could get Minerva to jump into this water?"

Priscilla ran her long green fingernails through her jet-black hair. "One never knows what one can do until one tries," she cackled.

Priscilla took the water bowl out of Minerva's case. She held Minerva in her long bony hand near the water. Priscilla chanted another rhyme.

"Your life is safe in my hand. Jump now upon my command. Into the swirl, my little girl."

Before Ben's eyes Minerva crawled off

Priscilla's hand and fell into Sparky's water bowl.

"That's the coolest trick I've ever seen," Ben said after Priscilla picked Minerva out of the water bowl and put the spider back in her case.

"Look out!" Jane yelled. Sparky leaped over Annie's head and landed right smack dab in the water bowl. Water splashed all over Jane, Annie, and Ben.

"What is wrong with this crazy cat?" Ben asked.

Priscilla just smiled and lifted the dripping cat out of the water. Sparky purred as Priscilla held her close.

GRRRRRRRRR! HISSSSSSS!

"There are those weird sounds again," Jane told Priscilla.

Priscilla smiled. "My sweet Bruno must be nervous. I must go to him." Priscilla gave Sparky one last pat and rushed inside Hauntly Manor Inn.

"Did you see what Priscilla did?" Ben asked his sister. "Wasn't that totally cool?"

But Annie didn't answer Ben. Instead, she put her hand on Ben's shoulder. "I have some bad news for you," she said. "You can't enter the pet show."

7
Homework Spell

"What are you talking about?" Ben asked Annie.

Annie put her hands on her hips. "You can't enter these spiders in the pet show."

"Why not?" Ben asked. "I'm sure to win with the cool tricks they can do."

Annie shook her head. "These spiders have been put under a spell."

"A spell?" Ben and Jane shouted together.

"Annie's flipped her lid." Ben laughed.

"I have not," Annie said, stomping her foot on the Hauntlys' porch. "Didn't you hear Priscilla Pocus saying those weird rhymes?"

Ben and Jane nodded.

Annie pointed her finger at the spiders.

"That was Priscilla casting a spell on those poor little spiders."

Ben laughed. "If that's true, I want Priscilla to go to school with me. Maybe she could put a no-homework spell on my teacher."

Jane laughed, too, and slapped Ben's hand in agreement.

"This is not a joke," Annie said. "Didn't you notice how Priscilla was dressed? What kind of ordinary person goes around dressed totally in black and has weird green fingernails like that?"

Jane shrugged. "My cousin is from New York City and she dresses like that."

"This is not New York," Annie pointed out. "This is Bailey City and here people don't dress like creatures from the black lagoon."

Ben twirled his finger beside his head. "You're crazy. Having these spiders do tricks is the best thing that ever happened around here. You're just jealous because I'm going to win that new bicycle."

Annie stomped her foot again. "I'm telling you that Priscilla is dangerous. She is definitely a witch!"

"A witch?" Issy yelled from behind Annie. "Who is a witch?"

Jane jumped up from the porch. There on the sidewalk stood Issy. Her green parrot, Filbert, sat on her shoulder.

"Annie was just kidding around," Jane said. "She might be a witch for next Halloween."

"I thought she called someone named Priscilla a witch," Issy said.

"Jane is just being nice," Ben said. "But I won't be. Annie was calling you a witch!"

Issy's eyes got big. "You were calling *me* a witch?"

Ben folded his arms in front of his chest and nodded, but Annie grabbed Issy's wrist. "Don't get mad," Annie told Issy. "I was just joking."

Issy's face got bright red. "You won't be joking around when I win that new bicycle this weekend."

"You aren't going to win," Ben blurted out, "because I have a secret weapon."

"Shhh," Jane hissed, but it was too late. Issy was already looking at the spider cases.

8

Parrot-Eating Pet

"What are those disgusting little things?" Issy asked.

Ben pulled his shoulders back proudly. "Those are the pet spiders that are going to win the bicycle," he told Issy.

"Ben," Jane warned, "maybe you'd better keep quiet about that."

Issy just laughed and petted the parrot on her shoulder. "There's no way a bunch of bugs can beat my parrot."

"Spiders aren't bugs," Annie explained. "They're arachnids."

"And they are a lot smarter than your pile of stinking feathers. Just watch this," Ben said. Ben looked at the spiders and repeated Priscilla's words:

"Spinning webs and flies don't dread. Now, my sweeties, stand on your head."

As the four kids watched, the spiders flipped over on their heads. Even Sparky stood on her head. Issy's eyes got big and she gasped. "I knew something funny was going on around here. That chant was a magical spell."

Jane shook her head. "It's just a little rhyme that Priscilla Pocus chanted."

"It sounds like hocus pocus to me," Issy said. "Priscilla must have some kind of magical powers. This isn't normal."

"Neither are you," Ben said, "but we still let you hang around."

Issy put her hands on her hips. She started to speak, but the strange noise from Kilmer's basement stopped her short.

GRRRRRRRRR! HISSSSSSSSSSSS!

"Oh, my gosh," Issy squealed, and her pet parrot flapped his wings. "What was that horrible sound?"

Jane patted Issy's shoulder. "Don't worry. It won't hurt you."

"It might eat your parrot, though," Ben

said with an evil laugh. "That's Kilmer's parrot-eating pet."

"What kind of crazy place is this, anyway?" Issy said, her face turning pale. "The people who live here aren't normal."

"Welcome to Hauntly Manor," Boris Hauntly said, coming onto the porch with his wife, Hilda. Issy took one look at Boris' slime-green eyes and Hilda's wild hair and ran screaming down the street. Issy's parrot flapped its wings and perched on a dead tree branch in the Hauntlys' front yard.

"What a strange little girl," Boris said before he and Hilda went back into the house.

Jane grabbed Ben's arm. "We'd better go get Issy."

Ben shook his head. "No way. I'm glad she's gone."

"Don't you understand?" Jane explained. "If we don't get her, she's going to tell everyone that funny things are going on at Hauntly Manor Inn."

"You're right," Annie said. "She might

even tell everyone that Kilmer's family is a bunch of monsters."

"What can we do?" Ben asked.

"Don't worry," Annie said. "I have an idea."

9
Secret Weapon

"It won't work," Ben said bluntly after Annie explained her plan. Jane, Annie, and Ben still stood on the Hauntlys' front porch.

"It's kind of mean," Jane said.

Annie shrugged. "We'll only use it like a secret weapon if it's absolutely necessary to protect the Hauntlys and Priscilla from Issy."

"I guess it's worth a try," Jane agreed.

"What do we do first?" Ben asked.

Annie walked over to the Hauntlys' front door. "First, we ask for help," she explained and banged the knocker.

Slowly, the door creaked open. Priscilla Pocus stood in the doorway. Her black dress swirled around her feet and she brushed back her long black hair with green fingernails. "Hello, my pretty little ones," Priscilla said. "What can I do for you?"

"We were hoping you could help us one more time," Annie explained.

Priscilla laughed. It sounded like a witch cackling to Jane and it sent chills up her spine. "Would you like me to teach the spiders another trick?" Priscilla asked.

"Sure," Ben said quickly.

Annie frowned at him and shook her head. "Actually," Annie said, "we were hoping we could teach that parrot to say some funny words."

Priscilla took one look at the bright green parrot sitting on the dead tree limb and smiled. "It will be a pleasure," Priscilla said.

Priscilla pointed to the parrot and curled her finger before saying, *"Feathers flying all around. Come to me, on the ground."*

Immediately, the parrot flew to the porch and landed by Priscilla's feet.

Priscilla patted the parrot's head. "Now, what shall we teach the parrot to say?" Priscilla asked.

Ben grinned. "I have some good ideas about that."

The three kids giggled and Priscilla cackled as they taught the parrot some silly sayings. All it took was a little rhyme from Priscilla and the parrot was squawking anything they wanted him to say.

"This is fantastic," Jane told Priscilla.

"It's wonderful," Annie agreed. "Thank you, Priscilla."

Ben laughed. "I can't wait to see Issy's face when her bird squawks these sayings."

"Hopefully that will never happen," Annie reminded him.

"We better take this bird back to Issy," Jane said.

Annie nodded. "I'll do it," she volunteered. She carefully picked up the parrot and carried it on her arm to Issy's house.

Issy rushed out of the house and grabbed her parrot from Annie. "Oh, Filbert," Issy cried. "I thought I'd never see you again."

"You left him at the Hauntlys'," Annie explained.

Issy buried her face in Filbert's feathers. "I was afraid that crazy family might put him under a magical spell and turn him into a gorilla."

Annie giggled. "The Hauntlys are very nice. They would never do anything like that."

Issy stared at Annie. "The Hauntlys are strange, and if I didn't have to teach Filbert some tricks for tomorrow's pet show, I would do something about it."

10

Operation Parrot

"I'm going to win," Ben sang as he knocked on Kilmer's door. It was the next day and the pet show was only an hour away. Annie and Jane stood next to Ben on the porch. Annie carried a big bowl of water.

"Maybe Kilmer will win," Jane told Ben. "His pet sounds very unusual."

Ben shrugged. "It'll have to be fantastic to beat my acrobatic spiders."

"Those are Kilmer's spiders," Annie reminded him.

"I know," Ben said. "If they win, I'll let Kilmer ride the bicycle, too."

Kilmer opened the door to Hauntly Manor Inn. Kilmer always looked strange, but today he looked worse than usual. His shirt was ripped in several places and his jeans had more holes than a golf course.

"What happened to you?" Jane asked.

"Bruno," Kilmer said as he led his friends into the living room. "Bruno has been most uncooperative. He refuses to wear a leash and he's too big for a cage."

"Oh, my gosh," Annie said when she saw Kilmer's living room. The old couch was turned over and several chairs had the stuffing torn out. "Did Bruno do this?" Annie asked.

Kilmer nodded. "I guess I cannot enter the pet show," he said sadly.

"Why don't you enter Sparky?" Jane suggested.

"No," Kilmer said. "Sparky might eat Eddie's dog."

Ben gulped. "I can't believe I'm saying this. Why don't we share the spiders?"

Kilmer put his hand on Ben's back. "You would do that for me?" Kilmer asked.

"Sure," Ben said with a smile.

"Then let's get going," Jane said. To-

gether the four kids and the three spiders headed off toward Bailey City Park. Annie still carried the big bowl of water. Kilmer's cat, Sparky, trailed along behind.

Bright yellow and green balloons decorated the stage in the middle of the park. A huge sign said: PET SHOW TODAY!

"Look," Jane said. "There's Issy with her parrot."

Issy sat on a park bench beside a girl named Liza. Liza was brushing the hair of a little kitten. Eddie sat on the ground beside a huge Dalmatian. The dog licked Eddie's face.

"It looks like half of Bailey City is here today," Annie said, looking at the crowd of kids around the stage.

"It won't do them any good," Ben said smugly. "Kilmer and I have the pet contest tied up tight."

Finally, the pet show began. Eddie went first and his dog knocked down two of the judges. Liza's kitten was so scared, it jumped on a balloon and popped it. Issy's

parrot sat on Issy's shoulder and said, "Awwk!" Several other kids brought their dogs onto the stage and one kid even had a pet pig. Finally, it was time for the last contestant.

Ben grinned when his name was called. Kilmer and Ben carried the spider cases onto the stage. Annie put the water bowl beside the cases. Sparky sat on the end of the stage, behind Kilmer.

Ben whispered Priscilla's rhyme and waved his hands around.

"Spinning webs and flies don't dread. Now, my sweeties, stand on your head."

The crowd gasped as the spiders stood on their heads. Behind Kilmer's back Sparky stood on her head, too.

Ben smiled and said the other rhyme. Kilmer held Minerva in his hand.

"Your life is safe in my hand. Jump now upon my command. Into the swirl, my little girl."

Minerva crawled to the side of Kilmer's hand and fell into the bowl of water. As

the crowd cheered, Sparky leaped over
Kilmer's back and landed face first into the
bowl. Everyone in the crowd cheered. Ben
groaned. "Sparky, you better not have ru-
ined our chances to win."

"Oh no, my dear boy," said the head
judge. "On the contrary. We've never seen
a better-trained cat. Your cat has won first
place!"

Ben jumped and whooped. "Actually,
it's Kilmer's pet," he said when he finished
cheering.

Kilmer smiled as the judge wheeled out a brand-new shiny red bicycle. The crowd cheered.

"Don't worry," Kilmer told Ben. "We'll share it." Ben grinned and clapped along with the crowd.

One person in the crowd wasn't clapping and that was Issy. Issy was mad. She pushed her way through the crowd and stomped onto the stage.

"Oh, no," Annie said. "I think it's time for Operation Parrot."

11

Filbert Has His Say

Issy marched clear across the stage. Filbert clutched her shoulder, hanging on tight. With each step she took, Filbert's wings fluttered and slapped her on the head. Issy didn't stop until she reached the judge. She grabbed his sleeve and tugged.

The judge glanced down at Issy and her bird. "What seems to be the problem?" he asked.

"You can't give those monsters the prize," she said loud enough for her words to echo over the microphone. "I should get the bike because I worked hard at training Filbert."

"We worked hard, too," Ben said. "We trained Minerva, Elvira, and Winifred."

"But they had help!" Issy interrupted.

The judge scratched his chin. "I believe help is allowed," he told Issy.

"Not the kind of help I saw," she said. "It was definitely not fair."

The rest of the crowd was quiet as they waited for Issy to continue. Annie crossed her fingers and Jane gasped. "Ben better hurry up," Jane said, "before it's too late!"

Issy opened her mouth, but Ben spoke before she had a chance. *"Filbert was there. He knows what to say. He'll tell the truth, and right away!"*

When Ben uttered the words Filbert flapped his wings and hopped onto the judge's shoulder. "Awk!" Filbert screeched over the microphone. "Issy talks too much. Awk!"

The crowd giggled, but Issy's mouth fell open and her ears turned pink.

Filbert didn't notice. He squawked again. "Awk! Issy wears purple underwear. AWK!"

Now Issy's entire face was the color of a raspberry. Before Filbert could say another

word, Issy turned and raced off the stage. Filbert fluttered from the judge's shoulder and flew after her.

The judge looked at Ben and Kilmer. Then he looked at the rest of the audience. "My, my," the judge said. "I guess that bird can talk after all. I think Filbert and Issy deserve second place!"

The audience clapped, but Issy didn't come back to get her prize.

"We'll take the prize to her," Kilmer said. "We know where she lives."

"Thank you," the judge said. "But first, it's time for us to give you and Sparky your prize."

The crowd cheered as the judge gave Kilmer the shiny red bicycle.

"Wow," Ben said. "That is the coolest bicycle I've ever seen!"

Kilmer didn't say a word, but he definitely did not look happy.

12

Kilmer Makes a Deal

Ben was up early the next morning. He raced over to Hauntly Manor Inn on his old bicycle. Annie and Jane had to hurry to keep up with him.

Ben's bike used to be shiny black, but now it was covered with scratches and dents. He dropped his bike in the dead grass right next to Kilmer's new red one parked in front of the inn.

"I'm going to see if Kilmer wants to go riding," Ben said. "Maybe he'll let me ride his new bike."

Annie grabbed Ben's arm before he had a chance to knock on the door. "Are you sure Kilmer knows how to ride?"

"Of course he does," Ben snapped. "Everybody knows how to ride a bike."

"Don't be so sure," Jane said. "After all,

Kilmer didn't act too happy about it yesterday. He didn't even smile and he rolled his bike all the way home."

"Maybe he just felt bad about Issy," Annie said. "She really was embarrassed in front of everybody."

"We had to do it," Ben said, "before she told everybody about Priscilla Pocus. Besides, I think she felt better when we gave her the second place prize."

"I guess you're right," Annie said. "But Kilmer didn't try riding his new bike once."

"That's because we had our hands full," Ben said. That was true. The kids had to carry home the spiders and water bowl. "Kilmer's new bike is the best, and I'll prove it."

Before the girls could say another word, Ben lifted the giant tarnished door knocker and let it fall. They heard heavy footsteps echoing through Hauntly Manor Inn. Then the door slowly squeaked open and Kilmer peered out at them.

Ben smiled. "How about a bike ride?" he asked.

Kilmer shrugged, but he still didn't look very happy.

"Don't you like your new bike?" Annie asked.

Kilmer sighed. "It is a nice bike," he said sadly.

"Then what's wrong?" Jane asked.

Kilmer looked past his three friends and out into the yard. He smiled when he saw Ben's bike. "I just wish my bike were more like Ben's."

"WHAT?" Annie said. "His bike is scratched up."

"And full of dents," Jane added.

"Yes," Kilmer said. "It is the best-looking bike in Bailey City."

Jane, Annie, and Ben looked at each other and shrugged. "If you really like my bike better," Ben said with a grin, "I'll trade with you."

"Do you mean it?" Kilmer asked. "You would really take my new bike and let me have your black one?"

Ben shrugged. "Sure. After all, we are friends."

Kilmer jumped up and yelled. When he landed, the entire porch shook. "It's a deal," Kilmer said.

Just then, Sparky darted out the door. She skidded to a stop and arched her back. With her ears plastered back against her head, she hissed at Jane, Annie, and Ben. Then Sparky raced down the steps and disappeared around the corner of the house.

"I think Priscilla needs to remind Sparky to be friendly," Annie joked.

Kilmer shook his head. "Priscilla left last night," he said. "She likes to fly when there is a full moon. That way she can see better."

Then Kilmer followed Ben down the steps and they both hopped on their bicycles. Annie and Jane watched Ben race away on the shiny red bike. Kilmer followed him on the scarred black bike.

"I guess the magic spell is gone," Annie said. "It flew away with Priscilla."

"At least everything is back to normal," Jane said.

Annie pointed at the ground. Three hairy spiders crawled out of the inn and slowly climbed on Jane's sneaker. "With the Hauntlys as neighbors," Annie said, "things may never be normal again."

About the Authors

Marcia Thornton Jones and Debbie Dadey like to write about monsters. Their first series with Scholastic, **The Adventures of the Bailey School Kids,** has many characters who are *monsterously* funny. Now with the Hauntly family, Marcia and Debbie are in monster heaven!

Marcia and Debbie both used to live in Lexington, Kentucky. They were teachers at the same elementary school. When Debbie moved to Aurora, Illinois, she and Marcia had to change how they worked together. These authors now create monster books long-distance. They play hot potato with their stories, passing them back and forth by computer.

About the Illustrator

John Steven Gurney is the illustrator of both **The Bailey City Monsters** and **The Adventures of the Bailey School Kids.** He uses real people in his own neighborhood as models when he draws the characters in Bailey City. John has illustrated many books for young readers. He lives in Vermont with his wife and two children.